THE LAST
SNIFF

DR. DEEPAK PANCHOLI

authordeepakpancholi@gmail.com

BlueRose ONE.com
Stories Matter
NewDelhi • London

BLUEROSE PUBLISHERS
India | U.K.

BlueRose ONE
Stories Matter
NewDelhi • London

For permissions requests or inquiries regarding this publication, please contact:

BLUEROSE PUBLISHERS
www.BlueRoseONE.com
info@bluerosepublishers.com
+91 8882 898 898
+4407342408967

ISBN: 978-93-7139-923-4

Cover design: Daksh
Typesetting: Tanya Raj Upadhyay

First Edition: August 2025

Dedication

To my dear father Shri Balkrishna Sharma who introduced me to the great and beautiful world of literature by putting a pen in my hand. Also dedicated to all those helpless creatures of the world who feel that they are helpless but the Almighty God is their and all of us's support.

Foreword

In 1992-93, when I was studying in 12th class, after a long cold, I gradually lost my sense of smell. The sense of smell is important for a human being but it is not essential or desirable. I have been managing without it for the last 30 years and on some occasions it has also helped me to live in a place with a very bad smell, although the disadvantage is that now I can hardly feel the smell of flowers, the aroma of food etc. Around the year 2000, a thought suddenly struck my mind that a human being can survive even after having a bad nose, but what about the creature whose nose is completely dependent on it? At that very moment, the idea of the police sniffer dog "Ruchoo" came to my mind. In the Mewar region of Rajasthan, Ruchoo means a loving puppy of a dog. During that time, I started writing the story of "Ruchoo" but due to laziness and many other reasons, I could not complete it. After that in 2024, when I told this idea to my wife Suman, son Harsh and daughter Moomal, they suggested that the story should be expanded and given the form of a novel. During the same time, my senior colleague, retired English professor Dr. Khushwant Singh Kang proposed to translate some of my works into English, then the idea came to my mind to write a novel on "Ruchoo" and get it translated into English, and today its result is in your hands. Although my first story was published in the seventh class itself, my first novel came quite late. Painter Abhay Munshi has made a significant contribution in giving a tangible form to this novel; he has enhanced the beauty of the novel with his wonderful illustrations. My college mates, younger sister Professor Bharti Veerwal and Professor Anil Chuhadiya also contributed a lot in realizing this big dream of mine. I am also thankful to Assistant Professor Ritu Verma who, on my request, did the proof reading multiple times. At first glance, this novel may seem like a children's novel, but this novel is for readers between 8 and 80 years of age and undoubtedly once you start reading it, the child inside you will call out to you again with a deep confidence. And if that happens, it will be a dream come true for me as a writer.

Translator's note

Since ancient ages man has shown tendency to learn from the fables in which different characters are assigned to various animals. In fact they were one of the prime source to teach moral values to children as they were fables which are tales with a moral purpose as in Panchtantra and Aesop's Fables teaching hoary wisdom to the readers since time immemorial. This book in the hand is also a similar purpose to teach various moral values mostly to school going kids that why illustrations have also been put in the book. I hope this effort will benefit readers irrespective of class, gender and age some of the traits of the protagonist embody moral values of universal significance. Readers will find this work a whiff of fresh air in the suffocating age of moral crisis, particularly in the young people. Any comments and precious suggestions to improve this effort are welcome as this work is not the end rather it is just a beginning as author intends to bring out many such works in future too.

- Dr K. S. Kang

The Last Sniff

Only some creatures in this world are fortunate, and among them, beasts are rarer. One such fortunate creature was a dog named Ruchoo. Though it was not a foreign breed, but due to its strong and unique sniffing power that it is a favourite crime buster and investigative canine of the Police Department. Ruchoo had been working with the Police for the last couple of years and, due to its powerful olfactory sense, had helped the Department to solve many cases and nab the criminals, and put them behind bars. Though there were other dogs also in the department and some of them were even of a foreign breed, like Sheru and Jabanj, but due to some unique attribute, Ruchoo had become the favourite hound of the Police that even made his fellow dogs, Sheru and Jabanj, envious. But life does not remain smooth and swift. There are ups and downs in life, rather it is like a wave full of ups and downs, and these ups and downs are part of everybody's life, whether it is a human being's life or the life of this dog Ruchoo.

One fine morning, Ruchoo was enjoying the warmth of sunlight on a moderate winter while its colleagues- Sheru and Jabanj- were whispering something in a corner. Suddenly Ruchoo's trainer Ramdin came in quick strides and, waving his hand of affection on Ruchoo's back, took it to a scene of crime and Ruchoo too responded to Ramdin's gestures showing affection by embracing Ramdin's legs with its paws. Then starts the process of identifying the criminals by sniffing the spot of the crime.

The spot of crime was a room where a corpse of an old man was lying in a pool of perhaps his blood, and the things in the room were lying scattered, indicating a gruesome struggle before death. Taking Ruchoo near the dead body, Ramdin commanded Ruchoo 'Sniff and find' and then Ruchoo's work began in earnest. Police had already surrounded the scene of the crime. As Ruchoo was sniffing clothes, a dead body, and other things in the room Policemen looked hopefully at Ruchoo. After sniffing the clothes of the dead old man, Ruchoo barked and ran towards the open window in the room, which was an indication that the culprit had escaped that way after committing the crime.

In an instant, Ruchoo jumped through the window and was moving towards a particular direction while Ramdin and the other policemen followed Ruchoo closely. Finally, Ruchoo entered a narrow lane and stopped before a two-storey house. Policemen and Ramdin, following Ruchoo, too, stopped. Soon, there were policemen around that house while four constables and Ruchoo entered the house. Stopping before a room, Ruchoo started barking loudly. Soon, three armed people came out of the room. Policemen were already prepared for this situation, and then began the Police's encounter with the culprits. Soon, policemen succeeded in rounding up two criminals, and as the third one was trying to escape, Ruchoo jumped at him suddenly. Taken aback, this fellow ran towards the door and, finding policemen waiting for him at the entrance of the building, he turned back towards the room and faced Ruchoo's assault once. Though he succumbed before Ruchoo but before that he succeeded in stabbing Ruchoo in its nose with his dagger, due to which Ruchoo was bleeding profusely from the nose. Ruchoo was taken to the hospital quickly. Vet Doctor bandaged its bleeding nose and gave Ruchoo an injection. For the next couple of hours, Ruchoo was recovering from this injury that had been inflicted by the criminal in the last encounter. But nobody was aware of the great change that was going to come in Ruchoo's life soon.

One day, as usual, Ramdin, Ruchoo's trainer and caretaker, came and took Ruchoo to the shop of Fakir Chand, which had been burgled and broken into by the thieves. Ruchoo knew very well that its job was to identify the culprits by sniffing things in the shop. 'Sniff' commanded Ramdin to Ruchoo, and Ruchoo, who had helped police several times in putting criminals behind bars, started sniffing the things in the shop, but to his utter surprise, it was unable to detect any smell in the things that it sniffed. It soon dawned on Ruchoo and other policemen that due to its nasal injury in the last encounter with the criminals, it had lost its sniffing power. And a dog, especially the investigative dog of the police department, was worthless without the sniffing sense. Perhaps the stab of the knife on its nose that was given by the criminal in its bid to escape the police had permanently injured its olfactory sense. Ramdin and other policemen were utterly surprised to find that Ruchoo was unable to detect anything from the things lying scattered in the shop. Lying helplessly at the feet of Ramdin, tears came to the eyes of Ruchoo as it was unable to give any clue about the crime to the waiting policemen.

The inspector ordered Ramdin to take Ruchoo to the Vet Hospital at once, and he also ordered Ramdin to bring other dogs- Sheru and Jabanj- to the scene of the crime.

Veterinarian Dr. Durbal Singh, after examining Ruchoo, diagnosed that Ruchoo had lost its sniffing power forever due to the nose injury incurred by a stab from a knife by the criminal. This fact stunned Ruchoo as it appeared to be the saddest day of its life. Ramdin was also upset at getting this news as he had grown attached to Ruchoo due to his long association with it, that he almost considered Ruchoo as a member of his family, and just like one of his sons. As Ruchoo had become worthless for the police department so it did not take long to get rid of this liability and issued orders to release Ruchoo from the services of the department at once, following the dictum of 'no work, no pay'. All the efforts of Ramdin to retain Ruchoo proved to be futile, as he was concerned about the well-being and security of his dear Ruchoo. Even the Municipality was not ready to take it so that two square meals of the day could be secured for Ruchoo. Ramdin was unable to take

Ruchoo to his house due to his dominant wife, Usha, who had an aversion to dogs, as one of them had bitten her during her childhood.

When Ramdin brought Ruchoo to his house, his wife burst out, losing her temper, saying, 'We are unable to bring our kids and make both ends meet on your meagre salary, how can we afford to keep this worthless creature. But still he made a meek effort by saying, 'Don't say so dear, Ruchoo is a very sweet creature and even our kids are also much attached to it, and then it will not prove too costly for us, as whatever is left over from our food will be taken by Ruchoo'. But Usha gave an ultimatum, almost shouting, mad with rage, 'I don't want to hear anything, either I or Ruchoo will stay in this house, the choice is yours'. So, Ramdin was utterly helpless and had no option but to leave Ruchoo on its own to survive in the world. Even Ramdin's kids wanted to keep Ruchoo in their house, but they were also totally helpless before the ultimate of their mother.

Now Ruchoo, who had been living in comfort and luxury so far, was not even considered eligible to stay in a nook of an ordinary house. Now, time had completely changed as Ruchoo was in total dark where to go or what to do after leaving Ramdin's house. It was getting dusk when Ramdin ordered Ruchoo to leave his house, and he came into the street. As Ruchoo was not feeling very hungry at that time so it wandered in the streets. The time had come now to face and encounter the harsh realities of life and its bitter struggle for survival. Well-known scientist Darwin had given the theory of the 'Survival of the Fittest' a couple of centuries ago, as the creature survives successfully that can adapt according to the changed circumstances. Nearly such a situation has come for Ruchoo too, as it did not know that such a time would come when it would be without food or shelter, even though it has spent its life in comfort and luxury so far. It was a moderate winter evening, and soon darkness descended and took everything in the town in its embrace. Even the street lights were not able to give much illumination due to the bird's nest and other trash deposited on the bulbs of the streets of the town, and authorities have not cared to maintain or clean them or replace fused bulbs once they had been put up on the poles. Due to continuous wandering, Ruchoo was now feeling tired, so it decided to take some rest at the end of a street. But the moment it lay down, three dogs came at him barking ferociously as they did not want to share their area with Ruchoo. For an instant, Ruchoo thought to give a befitting reply to these dogs, but then, to avoid needless struggle with them, decided to withdraw peacefully, and Ruchoo walked out of the street. While coming out of the street, Ruchoo was sadly thinking about these three dogs who were disillusioned and were ready to shed blood for their so-called area. The reality of life was that nobody, including these three stray street dogs, would be able to retain an area forever in life. So, it was futile to fight for the area. They do not know that even the area they claim to be theirs will not remain with them forever, as Ruchoo considered the Police Headquarters as its area, but he was thrown out of it in an instant. These three ignorant dogs did not know that any mightier creature than them can drive them easily from their area, or any day municipal authorities may catch them and evict them to some remote forest from where they may never return. Then why this illusory possession of a particular area as their own.

The other end of the street ended on a highway on which vehicles-two wheelers and four wheelers-were plying speedily in their eagerness to reach their destinations. But Ruchoo was moving slowly, in comparison with the vehicles, like a tortoise aimlessly, as it had no shelter to rest. Under an overbridge on the highway, a Rickshaw was standing in the dim light of the street light. On the left of the cycle rickshaw, a bull was resting under the lamppost. Ruchoo was eyeing a vacant spot near the bull to spend the night. Ruchoo was unable to recollect any time in its life when it had to spend the night in the open in such untidy surroundings. Ruchoo had to struggle even for this untidy place to rest for the night. Such is the cruel game that fate had played with it. As Ruchoo moved towards this spot bull shook its horns threateningly towards it, indicating that Ruchoo should not dare to think of coming to that place. Seeing the large, sharp horns of the mighty bull, Ruchoo thought it safe to withdraw, and he succumbed to the bull's threat with a weak growl that awakened the rickshawman, who, clad in a shady holed vest and striped pants, was sleeping on the seat of the rickshaw. The spectre thin rickshawman was from Bihar, whose voyage in the land of dreams was disturbed by the growl of Ruchoo. On hearing the growl of Ruchoo, the frustration of abuses and insults hurled at him day long by passengers and traffic policemen erupted in the form of abuses for Ruchoo in his local dialect. A poor man vents out his anger and frustration, experienced by him throughout the day, on a person weaker than him. Here, his anger burst on poor mute Ruchoo, well knowing that this dog would not reply. Ruchoo was unable to comprehend the volley of abuses fired at it by the rickshawman. Taking it to be the worst day of its life, Ruchoo took it calmly and resolved to leave that place at once. As it started to move, Ruchoo heard the voice of the rickshawman beckoning it towards him. The rickshawman got up from the Rickshaw, as his sleep was disturbed, and took some water from a bottle. Suddenly, pitying Ruchoo, the rickshawman gave half a roti from his leftover dinner. Coming to the side of the Rickshaw, Ruchoo took the roti gratefully as it was nectar and manna for it. There were tears in its eyes while taking that half-roti. Ruchoo did not know that it would have to go through several phases of difficult times and struggles shortly, and it would have to adapt and adjust to the changed circumstances.

The rickshawman patted Ruchoo by moving his hand over its head with affection and allowed it to sleep under the Rickshaw. As night had fairly advanced, so the traffic on the overbridge had thinned as fewer vehicles were moving on it. Bull was also dozing off by hanging its head on one side. The rickshawman also started snoring within five minutes as he was dog tired after a hard work of whole day. The sleep that is 'balm of nature' gives comfort to the rich and the poor alike without any discrimination. But Ruchoo, due to hunger, was unable to sleep soundly, but a time comes in the night when sleep conquers all, including hunger, and that happened with Ruchoo too, as after midnight, sleep defeated hunger in this strange tug of war. After midnight, the three- Ruchoo, the rickshawman, and the bull were sleeping peacefully at their respective places in the sweet region of sleep. Once you enter the arena of sleep, the difference between the Kingly palace, a poor man's hut, and even the road is erased. Everywhere there is a reign of comfort and peace till the Sun uncle rises in the east in the morning.

In the far eastern horizon, the divine aurora was visible, and people and traffic had started moving sparingly on the road. Old, religious-minded minded pious women were moving towards the temple for their morning prayers. A newspaper hawker passed just by the side of the rickshaw, ringing the bell of his cycle and singing a popular Bollywood song. The sound of the bicycle bell had woken Ruchoo as it signalled another day-long encounter with the cruel, hard world for its survival. The rickshawman had woken up early in the morning to complete his morning rituals and ablutions in time to get early passengers in the morning to ensure that he gets adequate income during the day to enable his large family living in the far-off village to make both ends meet easily. Ruchoo looked towards the lamp post and found that the bull had disappeared from the lamppost. Earlier, the morning used to be mile and biscuit time for Ruchoo, but now, in changed circumstances, it was even beyond the dream to imagine such a thing. Ruchoo was unable to decide what to do next. So, it decided to sit leisurely under the rickshaw for some more time till the sweepers came and forced it to move from its place with their sharp and hard bamboo brooms. Ruchoo also saw that these sweepers were pointing their brooms threateningly at the rickshawman, forcing him to move his rickshaw from that place.

After a brief argument, rickshawman moved his vehicle from that spot, and while moving his vehicle his eyes met the eyes of Ruchoo and Ruchoo saw a strange attraction in the eyes of the rickshawman, so it came out from under the Rickshaw and stood near the legs of the rickshawman, wagging its tail with affection as it used to stand near the legs of Ramdin earlier. The rickshawman patted Ruchoo's head with affection in return, which indicated that the day had begun on a favourable note, though still it could not get anything to fill its tummy, but Ruchoo had succeeded in getting precious affection from somebody in this cruel, hard, and strange world. The sun had come into the sky, and it was again ready to commence its countless marathons of the day. The harsh sound of vehicles plying on the road warned Ruchoo to be ready for the day-long struggle. Soon, the traffic over and under the bridge increased. Ruchoo was feeling the sharp pain of hunger in its belly by this time, and it came to a vendor selling tea, poha, and other edibles. Hunger forced Ruchoo to move towards the Vendor's shop. Near the Vendor, three to four people were sitting on rickety, feeble chairs, sipping a hot cup of tea. One plump man, smoking a cigarette, was discussing the menace of rising pollution in the town. Five to seven people were surrounding the cart of the Vendor, demanding Poha, which was an indication that this man prepared good and healthy snacks for morning breakfast, and he was quite popular with his customers. If Ruchoo's nose had been normal, it would have enjoyed the sweet aroma of the edibles, but it was utterly helpless. Guided by hunger as Ruchoo came near the Vendor's cart, a man protested and asked the Vendor to shoo away the stray dogs from this place so that they could take their breakfast in peace. The very next moment, the Vendor gave a sound kick to Ruchoo that made Ruchoo wince with sharp pain as the attack was sudden and Ruchoo was not ready for it. Due to this sudden and unexpected attack, which had hurt his mind and soul more than the physical hurt, forced to move away from that place at once. Ruchoo did not remember any moment in its life when it had received such a humiliating and insulting kick from anybody.

Saddened and disappointed, Ruchoo moved away from that spot at once. While coming, a child's voice fell on Ruchoo's ears, who had come to buy snacks with his father, saying, 'See Papa, what a grand hound, why not take it to our house?'. On hearing these words, Ruchoo stopped at once, hoping that it would finally get a permanent shelter again, and it even came towards them wagging its tail. But suddenly man replied, 'No, my dear son, we cannot take any stray street dog to our house'. With that, Ruchoo's skyscraper of hope of getting permanent shelter dashed to the ground at once. Ruchoo could not prove to the father-son duo that it was not an ordinary dog of the street. The very next moment, it came into its mind that even if it had been an ordinary stray dog of the street, nobody could have taken away the 'Right to Live' from it. The Almighty must have created the entire universe with some rationale, but ignorant and foolish man weighs everything on the scale of selfish interests. A line of hatred appeared briefly on Ruchoo's face as it started moving away from that place without looking back. For the next couple of hours, Ruchoo wandered in the streets like its fellow beings. Now hunger was troubling Ruchoo, which sharpened when he saw people eating things at various places.

After moving on the highway for quite a long time, it moved into a narrow street lined with large rows of houses situated on the sides. Seeing it, Ruchoo smiled at the thought that if man had the power to encroach, he would have swallowed up the entire street. As Ruchoo crossed the couple of houses, a girl's voice fell on its ear, who had perhaps come to throw a cold, stale piece of bread. Moved by hunger, Ruchoo reached near her promptly, and the girl threw the bread at it, apprehending that it might bite her. Ruchoo saw the roti lying in the dust and put its nose instinctively, but then it remembered that its nose is not working anymore, and that was primarily the cause of its misery. Ruchoo took that roti, which was eight to ten days old, as a layer of fungus had deposited on it. Ruchoo, despite the hunger, decided not to take that Roti and abusing the miser mistress of that house in its mind moved away leaving that Roti in the dust. The street was circular, but Ruchoo could not get anything to eat even after taking a round of the entire lane. Now it appeared to Ruchoo that it had committed a folly to leave even that cold, stale, contaminated piece of bread as it was now no longer the privileged and trained dog of the Police Department of some elite dog of a millionaire living in a palatial mansion, so now it cannot afford to make choices or show attitude. Its condition was quite similar to the state of a beggar who could not make any choice and must accept whatever he gets. Now it was high time that it should accept the reality and adapt itself to per new changed circumstances. So, Ruchoo once more turned towards that house, where the little girl had thrown it, but to its utter surprise, it had already been taken up by a cow. So, Ruchoo could not do anything except lament the lost opportunity. The Sun was shining in its full splendour in the sky, and Ruchoo, spotting a shadowy corner, decided to rest there for some time. But hardly had Ruchoo made itself comfortable at this spot when a pebble thrown by a mischievous school boy hit it, causing sharp pain in its leg. Perhaps these school-going kids were practising their aim, or perhaps taking revenge for their thrashing they received by them at their homes by their parents at the school by their teachers. Ruchoo, in pain and anger, moved quickly towards the kid, and taken aback by that unexpected attack, the kid moved back and lost his balance and fell on the ground, and panicked, and started yelling at once. Seeing a child fall on the ground, a couple of men shooed away Ruchoo and said,' These street dogs are getting aggressive day by day. Municipal workers are too worthless to do anything effective to rescue people from stray dogs. Another fellow added while aiming a pebble at Ruchoo,' these stray curs have made lives of common people difficult'. Seeing the pebble coming towards it, Ruchoo thought it wise to retreat, and so it turned around. Ruchoo was unable to comprehend why human beings do not accept their follies. If it had a choice, it would certainly not have wanted to become such a human being who cannot accept their mistakes and punish the real culprits and do justice.

At the turning of the next street, a voice of a child fell on Ruchoo's ears saying, 'Oh! Ruchoo, certainly it is our Ruchoo'. Ruchoo turned to see a group of kids coming from the school, as the joy of learning could be discerned easily on their faces. These words consoled Ruchoo a lot; at least there was somebody in this cruel world who owned it. As kids came near Ruchoo, it could easily recognize that the boy taking its name was none other than the kids of its former master Ramdin- Ronak and Rahul, who came occasionally to see Ruchoo in Police Lines. Ruchoo and Rahul fondled Ruchoo by moving their hands on the head of Ruchoo, and it returned their affection by wagging its tail vigorously. Other kids were also encouraged to touch Ruchoo, though with some fear. Randin's elder son, Ronak, was telling his friends, 'Do you know we wanted to keep Ruchoo with us, but our mother did not budge.' One of the kids, too, added sadly, 'Yes, my mother, too, does not like canines'. Suddenly, Ramdin's younger son Rahul took out a tiffin box from his bag and placed the leftover food-half roti and some vegetable-from his tiffin before Ruchoo. All the Children understood at once that Ruchoo was hungry, the way it ate eagerly. But with that, an idea also came to them that they can conveniently escape scolding from their mothers at home for bringing unfinished tiffins from school by giving the leftover food to Ruchoo. Other kids also offered leftover meals from their tiffin boxes that Ruchoo accepted with pleasure and gratitude. Soon, a couple of hounds appeared, only God knows from where, and threatened Ruchoo, but they were driven away by the children. Ruchoo now had nearly its fill, and now it was ready to struggle for the whole day. Kids continued to play with Ruchoo till a warning voice of a lady- perhaps mother of one of the kids – was heard that dispersed the kids with fear that if they will get late in reaching their homes there is possibility of getting a sound thrashing from their mothers and as they had enough of thrashing already at school today, so they were in no mood to get one more thrashing. So, they moved quickly to their houses by bidding farewell to Ruchoo, but with a promise to meet again in the evening.

Ruchoo stayed there for some more time till a couple of street dogs came barking at him claiming their hold over that area, as Ruchoo was not in mood to fight so it moved away towards the main road where a crowd had collected as it seemed two bikes have collided and both the bike owners were arguing with each other to the amusement of the watching crowd. Ruchoo too stopped to watch the scene when the Police Van, hooting its siren, arrived on the scene of the accident. The sound of the hooter was a familiar sound for Ruchoo, and that sound reminded it remember the times when it used to go with pride in the Police Van to round up the criminals. The next moment Police Van stopped, and a couple of Cops came out of the van and started dispersing the crowd. A Police Sergeant, sitting in the van, was saying, 'We would have reached the scene of the crime long ago, but we have been delayed due to this idle crowd who have no other work but to watch the quarrel of the people.

Ruchoo saw its former colleagues Sheru and Jabanj sitting in the rear cabin of the police van. Both of them smiled with vanity and reproach at Ruchoo as Ruchoo was now a common street dog in their eyes, while they were specialised trained dogs of the department. Ruchoo had no option but to acknowledge the reality, but there was a time when Ruchoo looked down upon both of them and prided itself in its special sniffing power. Ruchoo had comprehended perfectly well that time is the most powerful force in the world. With embarrassment and humiliation, Ruchoo threw one last look at the van carrying Sheru and Jabanj. Both the constables, after clearing the crowd while returning to the van, noticed and recognised Ruchoo at once. One of them uttered in sympathy, 'Poor Ruchoo, let us give it something to gobble.' Though they called Ruchoo, Ruchoo with injured and hurt dignity, considered it proper to move away from that place by ignoring them.

After moving a few yards, Ruchoo turned onto a street, fearing that if it remained on the main road, it might have to encounter the police van again as it avoided humiliation before Sheru and Jabanj. Ruchoo had been a detective dog, though it had lost its sniffing power, but still it was a trained dog of the Police Department and so full of other virtues like keen observation, sharp ears, and a quick eye. Ruchoo was observing the streets that contained the house of his former master Ramdin, besides other houses and the highway, keenly, as it considered this to be its area of responsibility, as it had to remain there till it got some stable and durable shelter. After crossing a narrow and vacant lane as it prepared to enter the adjoining street, it was greeted by three to four spectre-thin dogs who came at it barking ferociously suddenly as if giving warning and throwing a challenge to Ruchoo.

Barking of the canines broke the silence of the street as it was the time of the afternoon when children and housewives were busy either in taking afternoon siesta or on their mobile phones, and menfolk had gone to work. Ruchoo was slightly upset at this sudden disturbance in silence caused by the barking of the street hounds, and at the same time, it smiled at the foolishness of these dogs and the entire Canine world of their tendency to control an area. One of the dogs who appeared to be the leader of the gang moved firmly towards Ruchoo, warning Ruchoo by keeping its tail straight. Ruchoo did not move or show any reaction to their barking, but still it was alert, though these four spectre-thin curs of the street were unable to do any real harm to it. They were unable to understand why Ruchoo did not move even after their ferocious barking, and now their leader was confused about how to deal with the situation. Normally, in such a situation, a fight ensues, and the vanquished side has to retreat with tails folded between their legs. But Ruchoo was neither taking up their challenge by commencing the fight nor it was succumbing before them and nor did it show any fear of its rivals. It appeared to them as if Ruchoo was making fun of them by completely ignoring their identity. In enthusiasm, a dog advanced towards Ruchoo while other dogs barked at it loudly, so it occurred to Ruchoo that the continual barking may disturb the peace of the residents, and if they come onto the street, then all of them will have to run away. So, Ruchoo straightened its body, took a step back, preparing to assault the advancing cur, opening its jaw fully and growling dangerously at this hound. This step forced the advancing cur to retreat with its tail folded between its legs it went behind its leader. In a few seconds, the battle ended as these four spectre-thin street dogs considered it prudent to withdraw. As Ruchoo did not intend to set up its control over that area, nor did it want to drive away these dogs from that area, so Ruchoo walked away before them like a victor, keeping its tail straight before these dogs. These curs were unable to understand why, despite winning the battle, Ruchoo had walked away like a victorious General, and they watched submissively the regal gait of Ruchoo as it marched before them.

As the Sun moved towards the western horizon, it was time of evening and time of playing for the children, who came out of their houses and moved towards the playing ground, though over the years number of children playing in the ground had declined sharply due to mobile addiction of the modern times. Ruchoo took the victory lap after its first triumph in the streets aimlessly, and as it was tired, it decided to take a nap under a car parked in front of a house situated in the street that also had Ramdin's house in it. A sweet brief cat nap took out weariness from the body, and the familiar voices of children going to the playground awakened it, and it felt energised and fresh after the brief nap.

'Today, I'll bat first, as I own the bat,' said Randin's elder son, Ronak, gleefully, by moving his bat in the air proudly before his friends.

'It means that you will not respect the outcome of the toss,' chipped in another boy as he wanted to challenge Ronak half-heartedly as his wavering voice was barely supporting his views, over the age-old convention that 'whoever owns the bat, will bat first'.

'Bro is right, we'll bat first' added Ramdin's younger son Rahul backing the views of his elder brother and put forward his claim by saying, 'I am the youngest so I'll bat first'. Thus, Rahul used the trump card of being the youngest in getting batting first as it was another unwritten law among the children that the younger kids should get the opportunity to bat first.

'Okay, but first of all, let us move towards the playing ground rather than wasting time here.' Ronak gave a verdict, waving his bat in the direction of the playground.

As they reached the end of the street, Ronak and Rahul exclaimed, 'Oh! It is our Ruchoo, O' yes, see friends it is our Ruchoo.' All the children bounded with joy at seeing Ruchoo sitting at the end of the street. Hearing the voices of the kids, Ruchoo came near them, delighted at the thought that it was able to meet the kids within the span of four to five hours. Ruchoo, wagging its tail, was moving around the legs of Ronak and Rahul affectionately. One little boy also wanted to touch Ruchoo, but he was unable to muster enough courage to do it. Reading the wish in his eyes, Ronak encouraged him by saying, 'Don't be afraid, it is our Ruchoo, it will not harm you'. In the next five minutes, all the kids got familiar with Ruchoo and were fondling Ruchoo by moving their hands on its back with affection. Thus began a new epoch of friendship between Ruchoo and the kids.

Ronak invited Ruchoo to join then for playing in the field by saying, 'Come on Ruchoo, let us move towards the ground to play the game of cricket'. So, all the kids walked towards the playing field in rapid strides and Ruchoo following them closely.

At one time, this ground owned by municipality was quite large but gradually it shrunk due to people's tendency of encroaching on public land. Today also in one nook of the ground cattle were grazing leisurely and in another corner a few children belonging to other streets were playing Cricket.

'Oh! It is our misfortune' wailed a child at seeing no place for them on the ground to play. All nodded in approval, but Ronak's keen eyes discerned a vacant corner in the ground, and if the cattle are dispersed, they will get an adequate place to play. All children again nodded their heads in approval, but who will bell the cat, that is who will make the effort to drive the cattle away from the ground. Before the kids say another thing, Ruchoo understood at once what was expected of it and commenced running towards the cattle in a threatening manner, barking at them loudly and furiously in its bid to become the hero of the kids by chasing away the cattle. Beasts grazing peacefully on the ground were taken aback by the sudden and unexpected assault, and they dispersed quickly. Their owner, busy on a mobile phone, chewing tobacco leisurely, came forward to drive back Ruchoo when he saw cows leaving the playground. But the cattle owner did not know that Ruchoo was an ordinary dog; it was a trained investigative hound. It could handle diverse situations, and it had even beaten lethal terrorists many times, so this tobacco-chewing cattle owner was nothing before it. When Ruchoo opened its jaw and jumped at the cattle owner, he fell to the ground, and his mobile phone fell out of his hand on the ground. he got up quickly and, turning, started following his retreating cattle without caring even to pick up his mobile.

'Oh, Uncle, at least take your mobile phone' called Ronak picking up mobile from the ground'. Dazed the cattle owner took his mobile from Ronak while keeping an eye on the movements of Ruchoo.

Kids got the space to play in the ground due to the courage and bravery shown by Ruchoo who had become hero for the Kids by this valorous act.

'This, your Ruchoo, is simply wonderful,' said a child.

To it, Ronak replied, saying gleefully with pride,' Were you taking me lightly? My father has trained Ruchoo. Rahul embraced Ruchoo, who was bounding with joy and sticking out his tongue in affection. After the ground was liberated from the cattle, it reverberated with the shouts of joy of the kids. As decided earlier, the team of Ronak and Rahul got the chance to bat first without caring for the toss. This undeclared law was quite effectively prevalent in small towns. During the game, Ruchoo stood at the corner of the field, and whenever the ball came towards it, it picked up the ball in its jaw and brought it back to the bowler promptly. It even caught a ball in its jaw once by diving and catching it in mid-air, making the ground echo with loud applause by the audience and players alike by saying, 'What a great catch?'. The players of other teams also applauded Ruchoo by saying, 'Great! This dog is a nice player.

Whose dog is it? I haven't seen it here earlier.' commented a grown-up player of the team playing near Ruchoo's team.

'Bro, this is our Ruchoo,' responded Ronak proudly, holding his claim over Ruchoo, and Ruchoo backed him up by wagging its tail.

'Bro, its name is Ruchoo,' added Rahul to show his presence and importance. Now Ruchoo had become a hero of the Kids playing on the ground, and even unknown children were coming to fondle and show affection to Ruchoo, and Ruchoo acknowledged it like a celebrity film star by wagging its tail and bowing its head before them.

Suddenly, one child, observing the setting Sun in the western horizon cautioned other children by saying 'now let us move towards our homes, as evening is about to descend soon.'

'Yea friends, we should start moving towards other homes lest our mammy will come,' said a little child with concern in his eyes that made Ronak smile and add, 'O' timid one, don't be afraid so much'. On hearing it, Rahul's eyes met with his elder brother Ronak, and he understood at once as he pointed in the direction of their houses to which they must start moving lest their mothers come and give them a sound scolding and thrashing on the ground itself before other people.

On getting Rahul's message in sign language, Ronak told the boys, 'Today, we enjoyed the game very much. Tomorrow we'll come early and play on the entire field.' Everybody nodded in approval and even Ruchoo wagged its tail to show its consent.

‘O’ Brother, will you take Ruchoo to your house?’ asked a boy who lived in Ronak’s neighbourhood. It was quite a serious issue as both Ronak and Rahul knew well that it was beyond their power to take Ruchoo to their home due to their mother’s intense dislike of the dogs. So, it was not only beyond their power but even beyond the power of their father to defy their mother by taking Ruchoo home. ‘Okay, first of all, let us start moving towards their houses,’ said Ronak to the children, though he knew very well that he would not be able to do anything about providing a permanent shelter to Ruchoo. Obeying Ronak children moved from the ground towards their houses in silence, with Ruchoo following them in the hope. Suddenly, Ronak asked the child walking beside him, ‘Oh, Himanshu, can you keep Ruchoo in your garage for the night?’.

‘Oh, no brother, my mother will turn me out of the house as she hates the dogs,’ dismissing Ronak’s proposal instantly, and Ruchoo’s hope of getting permanent shelter for a night at least was dashed to the ground. Ruchoo’s heart was at the breaking point once again. Turn by turn, all the proposals to keep

Ruchoo in their homes were turned down on one excuse or the other by the children. All children have left, leaving only Ronak and Rahul with Ruchoo. Addressing Ruchoo, Ronak said in a sad tone, patting Ruchoo's head,' Ruchoo, you sleep somewhere else today, tomorrow I'll make some arrangement for you certainly'. Both Ronak and Ruchoo knew very well that it was no solution, it was just a postponement of the problem, as tomorrow too, they will not be able to do anything about it. With these words, Ronak and Rahul entered their houses, leaving Ruchoo alone in the lane. There was silence in the street for some, and in the flickering lamplight of the street in the dusky evening was creating a scene of some horror Bollywood film was created. After some time, loud voices of arguments were heard from the nearby houses, which indicated to Ruchoo that it was now not proper to stay in the lane, and so it moved aimlessly towards the highway.

As Ruchoo came onto the main road, he remembered the rickshawman, and a ray of hope sprouted in his heart. Ruchoo soon reached the lamppost under the flyover and saw that the rickshawman was taking his evening meals on the seat of the rickshaw, and while eating, humming some tune of some folk song in his local dialect to entertain himself after a day of tiring work. Ruchoo heaved a sigh of relief on finding that today's bull was not there under the lamppost. As soon as the rickshawman saw Ruchoo, he invited it with affection to join him in his meals.

'Ae, ae, le, le, will you take something?' Responding to the rickshawman's invitation, Ruchoo came near him, wagging its tail in affection. Though the rickshawman had met Ruchoo only twice but he invited it to share meals as if it were an age-old acquaintance whom he had met after a long time. The rickshawman used to bring meals from the charity canteen that provided meals to poor people at concessional rates. Rickshawman placed a roti and some vegetables, leftover from his meals, on a paper before Ruchoo and fondled Ruchoo's head with affection.

'You take it, I'll just come after washing my hands,' instructed the rickshawman to Ruchoo as he left the rickshaw to clean his hands at the lamppost with a water bottle in his hand. Hungry Ruchoo took the meals with joy and gratitude. Suddenly, a car stopped on the overbridge, down came the windows, and some rotis were thrown out of it, and the car moved on. It was a jackpot for Ruchoo, who jumped at once to grab these chapattis gratefully and took them near the Rickshaw and started eating them. It appeared to Ruchoo that Almighty God, whom Ramdin used to thank frequently, was travelling in that car that brought these chapattis. Now, the rickshawman was lying on the seat of his rickshaw, gazing in turn at the sky and Ruchoo, turn by turn. By then, Ruchoo had finished its meals.

'You know, the firmament in our village is crystal clear and full of shining stars,' said the rickshawman, communicating his feeling to Ruchoo, as nobody was ready to listen to him as silently as Ruchoo, though Ruchoo could not make out what the rickshawman was trying to say. Copying the rickshawman's gesture, Ruchoo too started looking towards the sky.

Pleased with Ruchoo, the rickshawman spoke, moving his hand over Ruchoo's head with affection, 'You're a good friend.' Ruchoo was pleased to get this compliment and responded to him by moving its neck towards the rickshawman.

The rickshawman lamented with a heavy heart, 'Here you can see at most two or three stars in the firmament. What to do, friend, one has to leave their village to earn a livelihood and feed their family; otherwise, who wants to leave their native place?' He continued to stare at the sky for some more time in complete silence that was only broken by the humming of the insects.

He further said, addressing Ruchoo, 'Whenever I get the opportunity, I'll take you to my village, my younger daughter will be glad to meet you'. Now the weary rickshawman was descending into the peaceful dale of sleep and set on a timeless journey for the night. Night was getting cooler, and the rickshawman was still humming some folk song in his local dialect, Bhojpuri. In the next ten minutes, both the rickshawman as well as Ruchoo were embraced in the arms of sound sleep to the music of the humming insects.

Twittering of the birds woke both the rickshawman as well as Ruchoo early at 5 a.m. Stretching his body, the rickshawman looked under the rickshaw, addressing Ruchoo, 'Bro, sometimes it appears that night bridges the gap between the rich and the poor and it integrates them as both of them get the same peaceful, soothing sleep, that is balm of nature, without any distinction. Everybody gets peaceful sleep alike, whether he is a King living in a luxurious palace or a farmer living in hovels, or people like the rickshawman and Ruchoo sleeping on the ground. Sleep like balm of nature soothes everybody without any discrimination, but it is day that separates and divides humanity into various groups of the Rich and the Poor.' Ruchoo was listening to the rickshawman's harangue like an attentive pupil, though everything was getting over its head. But till the rickshawman continued his morning lecture,' this struggle and tiring race for survival and hard work to make both ends meet, is the creation of day, but you will not understand anything as you are fortunate that you are not a human and hence to you, poor or rich is nothing'. Closing his lecture, the rickshawman departed with a loud laugh at himself for addressing a mute animal as he left to finish his morning ablutions.

Lying under the Rickshaw, Ruchoo was thinking that its problems with the rising of the day began too, and some of its problems are identical with the problems of the human race, but even a human being cannot comprehend a dog's pain properly. For a few moments, Ruchoo recollected its comfortable past, but it wanted to forget its past as unsavoury as possible, as the sweet memories of its past were making its present life bitter. In the next hour, the rickshawman came back after completing his daily routine of morning ablutions and set out to work to get early traffic in the spirit of 'early bird catches the worm'. Ruchoo was hoping that the rickshawman would bring something to eat, and it too would get something out of that breakfast, but he did not have time and money to squander on breakfast. After taking the round of the overbridge, Ruchoo came onto the highway. It decided not to go to the snack vendor today, and so it moved just in the opposite direction to the snack vendor and wandered there aimlessly on the road for some time.

While moving aimlessly on the road, Ruchoo observed that on one corner of a street, an old crippled man with a hammer, anvil and nails, was squatting under a neem tree. He had come only a few moments earlier and was cleaning the space around him with a broom. Ruchoo saw to his surprise that this man swept the space in a sitting posture, and then the fact dawned on him that the man had no legs and was unable to take even one step on his own. On seeing the miserable state of this poor invalid man, Ruchoo forgot its problems for some time and, mustering courage, it moved closer to him. Seeing Ruchoo coming quite close to him, the old man was taken aback at once, but seeing a strange light of sympathy in its eyes, he did not drive it away. The old man gestured with his broom to Ruchoo to come near him and sit there. Ruchoo, who was now experienced in understanding the human language, knew it well that it was an affectionate invitation and not a sign of rejection. Like an obedient child, Ruchoo came near the old man and sat near him. This old invalid man, who was a cobbler, could read at once that Ruchoo was not an ordinary dog. Perhaps it belonged to some rich man and lost its way to its home. He allowed it to sit near him in the hope that if some rich man comes in search of his lost dog, then he may find it there and, on finding it there, haply this man may reward him adequately. Near the spot where Ruchoo was sitting, a heap of old and broken shoes to be repaired was lying. Seeing the heap, Ruchoo could see that this man was a cobbler by vocation, whose work was to repair the broken shoes and other footwear.

In the next half an hour, the cobbler shop became functional as footfall increased in the street with the advancement of the day. Over the last few years, when one could get shoes in shops and malls, the vocation of cobbler was on the decline as fewer people preferred their shoes to be repaired and reused. There was a growing tendency among the people to throw away the old shoes, instead of getting them repaired, and to buy new ones, which affected the cobbler's trade adversely. His only hope was people belonging to the lower middle class or lower class who still preferred to get their shoes repaired instead of replacing them with new ones. But then, poor people belonging to these classes had poor paying capacity, so they bargained hard on the cost of the repair.

Suddenly, Ruchoo looked up to a voice, 'O' Brother, my straps of slipper have come out, kindly fix them' demanded a middle-aged man, who was going to his work as a daily wage casual labourer. Throwing a glance at the slipper cobbler told this man, 'Repair will take five rupees.' Perhaps he was in a hurry to go to his job, so he cajoled the cobbler by saying, 'Okay, but please repair it quickly.' As this man took off his slippers, Ruchoo came forward before the cobbler or customer could get anything. It held the slippers in its jaws, placed respectfully before the cobbler as Ruchoo did not want the cobbler should drag himself forward to get the slippers and Ruchoo had done this work in an instant.

'Oh, this creature is quite intelligent,' uttered the middle-aged customer in surprise.

'So it is,' replied the frail old cobbler, moving one hand on its back with pride and affection.

After some time, the children started coming out of their houses as the school opening time was approaching. Some of them were riding bicycles while four to five of them followed them, discussing yesterday's cricket game loudly. All the voices appeared familiar to Ruchoo as he knew that among them were the sons of his former trainer, Ramdin. Ruchoo got up and moved towards the direction of the voices of the kids rapidly. Old cobbler was surprised at this sudden move of Ruchoo, but he was too engrossed in his work to react.

'Oh Ruchoo!'

'Our lovely Ruchoo.' Rahul saw Ruchoo first of all, and all the children surrounded it. Ruchoo was basking in glory like a film star acknowledging the greeting of its fans by wagging its tail vigorously.

'Kids, is it your dog?' asked the old cobbler.

'Uncle, it is not an ordinary canine, it is our hero Ruchoo,' said Ronak, moving its hand on its back with affection and pride.

'Then are you going to take it with you?' asked the frail, old cobbler with a tinge of sorrow and loss in his voice.

There was sudden silence on this query of the cobbler but recollecting his presence of mind Ronak replied, 'Uncle, at present, we are going to school, so you keep it securely with you, on returning from school we'll take it from you.'

The old cobbler nodded his head in consent and accepted the advise of the children, and the children were also happy that the cobbler had accepted the responsibility of keeping Ruchoo for a few hours.

'Come, Mr. Ruchoo,' the old cobbler welcomed him again. Ruchoo continued to watch the children till they disappeared when they turned into the lane of the school.

In the next couple of hours, only two customers turned up at the cobbler's shop; the rest of the time, both the cobbler and Ruchoo watched the people coming and going in the street.

After some time, the cobbler opened his tiffin and shared a roti and some vegetables with Ruchoo, and they both began eating simultaneously in perfect bonhomie. At the end of the meal, the old cobbler saved half a chapati and offered it to Ruchoo, feeling that he needed it more than himself, suppressing his hunger. Initially, Ruchoo hesitated to accept it, but soon hunger overcame his reluctance, and he gratefully accepted the chapati, reflecting on humanity.

He could not understand why the Almighty had created such diversity in human behavior among different people. Ruchoo finished the last piece of roti, casting a glance of gratitude at the cobbler, realizing that their conditions were almost identical. Ruchoo had reached this miserable state due to the loss of his sense of smell, while the cobbler struggled in life because of the loss of his legs. Yet, the cobbler had not lost the courage to fight against life's challenges, which is why a smile of contentment always played on his face.

Ruchoo shook its body and resolved to prove its worth again by overcoming its shortcomings. The cobbler took a catnap when he saw that there was no customer for a long time. Seeing him dozing, Ruchoo moved to take the round of three streets adjoining the highway in the hope of getting something to eat, as he was still feeling hungry. Shaking itself, it moved silently without disturbing the cobbler. Sniffing power, sharpness of ears, and knowledge of direction in a canine is far better and superior than in a human being. Though Ruchoo had lost sniffing power, but still police police-trained dog; it had other attributes as well. This highway and five to seven streets adjoining it had become practically Ruchoo's area. Ruchoo moved towards the street containing Ramdin's house, knowing that at that time only Ramdin's wife would be at home, as children would be at school and Ramdin at his workplace. The entire street was vacant, and there was no edible object visible anywhere in the lane. On the left side of the lane was Ramdin's house, where his wife, with a Roti in her hand, was waiting for the cow to come and take it. Ruchoo saw it with the hope of getting it and barked affectionately at her, but it enraged her, and she picked up a wooden stick to thrash it.

Ruchoo got it at once that it was not going to get that Roti, rather there are chances of being thrashed at the hands of Ramdin's wife. Besides a cow and a bull, the same one who was with Ruchoo at the lamppost, were coming quickly to take that chapati. So, Ruchoo thought it to be safe to come out of the lane. The situation in the next street was also the same, but Ruchoo saw a piece of stale chappati before one house. Perhaps the owner of the house had thrown it for the cow, but either the cow did not enter that street, or it could not spot it. So, Ruchoo took it as it had no other option at present. Ruchoo had not only to save its existence in these streets but also to maintain its control over this area so that no other hound may chase it from this area, as this area contained the house of its former master Ramdin as well as the house of his children's friends. As Ruchoo was eating the roti, the voices of barking dogs reached its ears. It appeared as if there was a bitter fight going on between two gangs of dogs. After finishing its meagre meal, Ruchoo decided to visit the next street to participate in the fight. When it entered that lane, Ruchoo saw that the gang of dogs, whom it had earlier vanquished, were struggling hard to save their area from a gang of seven to eight rival dogs. At that time, no human was visible on the entire street. Ruchoo stood aside for a few moments to watch the fight. The rival gang was not only more in number but in power as well. They had beaten a spectre-thin dog to the ground, who was lying in the dust while other dogs were protesting by barking ferociously. Ruchoo's keen eyes were observing everything, but still it was not able to decide whether to continue watching this fight as a mute spectator, as humans, animals, too tend to watch a quarrel, or to participate in the fight actively. At that moment, the leader of the losing gang approached Ruchoo, with its tail folded between its legs as if appealing to Ruchoo for help. Seeing the helplessness of this dog, who was bleeding profusely at the ears, as it had been bitten by the dog of the rival gang, the warrior in Ruchoo awakened and decided to help them, as Ruchoo had learnt during Police training that the weak and humble should be helped.

Ruchoo even forgot the fact that these were the same dogs who had challenged its authority by barking at it a few days earlier. So it moved towards the leader of the rival gang by barking loudly at it and assaulted it to rescue the spectre-thin dog that was grovelling in the dust. And then forced the leader of the rival gang to retreat by its attack with its powerful paws. Due to this sudden onslaught from an unknown quarter, the rival gang was taken aback to see a sturdy dog supporting them. Ruchoo's onslaught raised the morale of the local gang and forced the outsider dogs to retreat. Within five minutes, they not only beat the rival gang but the opponent team left the field submissively by folding their tails between their legs.

Ruchoo showed its grating teeth as a warning to the retreating gang not to make any such attempt in the future.

Local dogs got it at once that the dynamic leadership of Ruchoo had enabled them to score a victory against such powerful rivals. So, they accepted Ruchoo as their natural leader and surrounded it and showed their gratitude by bowing their heads and wagging their tails. Though Ruchoo was happy at this triumph but it was not in any mood to get involved with them by becoming their leader or boss of that area. After sinking the joys of victory for some moments and local dogs saw it walking regally like a victorious general after a mute, unsigned treaty with them that whenever they were in trouble, Ruchoo would come to help and protect them. The team had already acknowledged Ruchoo as their hero and natural leader. Taking the victory lap around the lanes, Ruchoo found bread and biscuits, thrown by a little girl as the war reward.

After the victory lap, Ruchoo came back to the cobbler's shop, who had awakened and was repairing the sandals of a lady.

'These days, companies are not manufacturing sturdy footwear as in bygone times,' the lady customer was complaining to the cobbler.

To it, the old cobbler replied in the affirmative by saying, 'Very much correct.'

When Ruchoo came near the lady, she was quite apprehensive and said, 'These stray dogs have increased in the town these days, drive them away.'

But the old cobbler replied reassuringly, 'Don't be afraid, Madam, it is my Ruchoo, a very sensible creature.' Cobbler gestured for it to come near and moved its hand with affection and commanded Ruchoo, 'Ruchoo, hand over these scandals to Madam'. Cobbler decided to exhibit Ruchoo's talent to this lady. Initially lady was fearful, but the sophisticated way in which Ruchoo picked up the scandals in its jaw and placed them respectfully before her impressed her immensely. She exclaimed in wonder and surprise, 'Oh! It is cleverer and more sensible than even my pet Tommy.' Ruchoo was quite pleased at getting this compliment and the packet of biscuits that it got as a reward from the lady as she departed after paying the cobbler. For Ruchoo, getting the compliment and reward of a biscuit packet from a lady was like getting a noble prize.

For the next hour, Ruchoo took a brief nap and then watched people and vehicles going on the road. The sound of the school bell fell on Ruchoo's ears, indicating the end of the school and his young friends would soon be meeting while coming from the school, so Ruchoo moved from that place to meet kids, as its joy doubled seeing the smiling and cheerful faces of children.

'Oh, lovely Ruchoo, you are waiting for us!' exclaimed Ronak at seeing Ruchoo coming towards him. Ronak stroked its head with affection. Ruchoo lifted its forepaws to embrace Ronak as other kids surrounded it. Passersby in the street were watching this scene with surprise. Some kids opened their tiffins and gave their leftover meals to Ruchoo so that it could have its fill, as today the quantity of food was more than yesterday.

'You know, today I demanded an extra chapati from my mom,' spoke Chintu, who was Ronak's neighbour, cleaning his specs.

Chintu, laughing at his cleverness, further said, 'I made the excuse that due to the tonic that I am taking regularly these days, my appetite has improved, so I feel hungry at school, so my mother put an extra roti in my tiffin. If I had said that I wanted this extra chapati for Ruchoo, she would never have consented to give it.'

'Hey, Chintu, do you think it is your idea? We also have implemented this plan already in our house, haven't we brother', chipped in Rahul, with Ronak nodding his head in consent. Now Ruchoo's tummy was full, and it experienced a new level of energy.

'Ruchoo, now we are going home, but after a couple of hours we will go to play on the ground, we'll take you too.' Rahul told Ruchoo as it expressed its approval by wagging its tail and lowering its head.

Now Ruchoo had to spend a couple of hours and decided to escort the kids up to their houses and wait for them at the corner of the lane till they came out of their houses to play cricket on the ground. Kids went inside their homes, and Ruchoo decided to take some rest by sitting under an electric pole. Ruchoo was about to doze off when a stone hit it in the stomach, causing it severe pain in the belly, accompanied by the sound, 'These stray dogs are becoming a menace in the town these days,' said a flat-faced man, who had thrown the pebble at it.

One of the two people accompanying him added, 'Yes, yesterday a stray dog bit a child in the nearby street'.

Writhing in pain, Ruchoo was wondering why it was being punished for the deeds of some other dogs. The third man, a rotund pot-bellied fellow, commented, 'These municipal workers are lazy, good-for-nothing fellows; they should be catching stray dogs, but they do not come.' Ruchoo decided to leave that spot as it knew very well that if it showed some reaction, then it would go against it, as human beings do not accept their mistakes easily. 'I'll talk to municipal authorities myself tomorrow and ask them to restrain these stray dogs and rescue citizens from their menace.' These words hit Ruchoo's ears more sharply than the stone as it left that spot, but it was filled with an apprehension of unformed fear. Ruchoo had been living with human beings for quite a long time, and its experience showed that if a thing is repeatedly said by human beings, it is sure to get implemented at least partially. Ruchoo had heard of the campaign of catching street dogs by the municipal authorities in the last few days, and it may soon start. This thought made Ruchoo uneasy and uncertain about its future as well as the future of other dogs of the street who were members of its team. In a couple of days, Ruchoo had succeeded in adapting itself to the changed and new circumstances of its life. But hardly had it grown comfortable with the new situation when this thought of being caught by the municipal workers and spending the rest of its life as a prisoner troubled it. Upset at this thought, Ruchoo took a quick round of the streets to locate a safe shelter during such an emergency. It met its team members, who showed respect to it by lining up in front of it respectfully like courtiers with their heads bent and tails down.

'How innocent are these stray dogs?' thought Ruchoo at seeing them standing in a line as if they were giving Ruchoo a guard of honour. It stayed with them for some time, but did not trouble them by leaving any trace of its current worry. A good leader never appears nervous and worried before his followers.

No animal harasses another creature without any rhyme or reason. The only two reasons that move a beast to harm other creatures are hunger or fear of security, and still, they call them street stray dogs. With these thoughts, Ruchoo came back to the old cobbler, who was also now preparing to call it a day by packing his shop and going home. As soon as cobbler left, the voices of kids coming out of their homes who were proceeding towards the ground to play cricket fell on Ruchoo's ears. Ruchoo at once came to know that the time to play cricket on the ground had come. So, leaving behind all apprehensions and fears, Ruchoo joined the lads with zeal. On the ground, Ruchoo was welcomed like a hero. Normally, three to four teams played daily on the ground, but today all of them decided to form one team and play all of them together. This change came only due to Ruchoo. Ruchoo's main benefit was that it was a good fielder and obeyed others' commands without any protest, and above all, it did not demand batting like other children. There were a few kids who would disappear after taking first on one or the other strange excuses. Ruchoo nearly played for two hours, leaving all the anxieties, fear, and apprehensions behind like all other beings on the ground.

'Friends evening is about to set in. Let us end the game,' said one stout boy, looking at the sky.

'Very true, otherwise an army of our mothers will appear with rolling pins in their hands and give us a nice thrashing,' said Rahul, smilingly, at which the whole ground echoed with loud collective laughter. In the next ten minutes, the ground was vacant and everybody was moving towards their homes. Ruchoo was following them silently.

'Friends, my mom was telling me that tomorrow municipal workers are coming to catch dogs. Is it true?' asked a boy to Ronak.

'My papa was also talking about the same thing on the phone with somebody,' said Chintu.

All these talks of the kids were troubling Ruchoo its safety and the safety of its team members.

Soon, all the kids forgot their joy and were lost in worries about the next day.

Showing concern, one kid said, 'What if they catch our dear Ruchoo?'

'No, we'll never let it happen,' said Ronak, though his voice shook, lacking confidence, which was easily discerned even by Ruchoo.

In the next few minutes, all children were inside their homes. At the turning of the street, Ronak threw a glance at Ruchoo as if asking Ruchoo to take shelter somewhere else. Ruchoo understood at once and started moving like an obedient child towards the overbridge. Children had already fed Ruchoo properly with biscuits and bread, so that its stomach was full at present. It decided to sleep under the rickshaw today as well. As it reached near the spot, Ruchoo saw the bull standing under the lamppost. Mustering courage, it moved near the Rickshaw, keeping a safe distance from the bull, but the bull did not react as it was busy with itself. Though the Rickshaw was there, the rickshawman was missing. Ruchoo was worried about him, and for the first time, Ruchoo felt the loss of sniffing power; otherwise, it would have easily traced him. Then a thought struck it that if its nose and sniffing power had not gone, it would still have been working as a privileged member of the Police Department. For the first time, Ruchoo felt helpless due to the loss of its sniffing sense. But this is life, if everything in life occurs as per one's wishes the life would become dull and monotonous. It appeared to Ruchoo that changed circumstances had made Ruchoo not only sensible but a philosopher too.

Sitting beside the Rickshaw, Ruchoo waited for the rickshawman. Its eyes met those of the bull. Today, the bull appeared to be in a good mood, but Ruchoo did not do anything to disturb so it moved its eyes from the bull, and saw the rickshawman coming, who appeared to be in quite a good mood, exclaimed. 'Oh, Babua, have you come? This time it had been a good crop in the village, and 'my wife has informed that hopefully this year moneylender's loan would be fully paid,' said the rickshawman to Ruchoo as if relating things to another human being who was listening attentively. He continued conversing with Ruchoo for nearly half an hour, listened to him like an attentive and sensible audience, and at intervals did not forget to nod its head in approval, though in reality nothing was going in its head.

In the sky moon had risen along with a few stars, and there was a pleasant and moderate winter evening that had made the entire atmosphere poetic. Traffic on the road had decreased, and the rickshawman from Bihar was humming a tune from a folk song in his local dialect. Wearied Ruchoo too was getting sleepy as the bull was munching peacefully, and when sleep overpowered rickshawman, his song stopped altogether. But as he was in a good mood today so whenever sleep broke, he resumed the humming of his song. Suddenly, three to four loud voices fell on Ruchoo's ears, indicating some crisis, so Ruchoo got up at once, though the bull was still munching unconcerned. The rickshawman, too, was sleeping soundly due to day-long, bone-breaking hard work.

'Oye rickshawman' shouted a fat, ugly man, shaking him vigorously. Another man added further, 'You are sleeping as if it is your grandfather's house, and that too before Jaggu Dada, you are sleeping peacefully while I am awake, this is my area, now cough out one hundred rupees quickly'. With that, he pulled the hair of the rickshawman who brought him out of sleep completely.

'Brother, I am a poor man, why are you troubling me?' pleaded the rickshawman meekly.

'Bugger, we know that you're poor, that's why we are demanding only hundred rupees lest we would have forced to fork out one thousand rupees from you', said the third man pushing rickshawman vigorously. Spectre thin rickshawman due to that push fell on the ground. As he fell on the ground, his eyes, showing his helplessness, met the eyes of awake and alert Ruchoo. Seeing injustice on a weak man awakened the soul of a soldier in Ruchoo. Though it had lost its sniffing power, the alertness, agility, strength, and good reflexes were in plenty in Ruchoo.

So very next moment, Ruchoo came out from under the Rickshaw to onslaught the person who had pushed the rickshawman to the ground and bit his hand. At this sudden attack from an unexpected quarter, this man got nonplussed and as he stepped back, lost his balance and fell on the ground with a resounding noise. By that time, Ruchoo jumped at the leader of the gang, Jaggu Dada, who tried to save him by throwing a bottle at Ruchoo, but the bottle missed Ruchoo and instead the bottle hit the head of his third man, and blood started flowing profusely from his head.

The fourth man, in nervousness, ran towards the lamppost, but the bull picked him up on its horns and threw him forcefully. As the situation had changed completely and left alone, Jaggu thought it wise to retreat, but only after he got a resounding kick from the rickshawman, and in his hurry to move away from that spot, he even dropped his purse.

'You've done well to save my dignity, Babua and the bull of Lord Shiva,' said the rickshawman to Ruchoo and the bull gratefully with tears in his eyes.

Picking Jaggu's purse, the rickshawman found an amount of two thousand rupees and decided to spend this amount on both of his companions- Ruchoo and the bull, who had come at the right moment to save his honour and dignity. Walking regally like a King around his rickshaw, the rickshawman sat on his seat, but then suddenly he got down and, embracing Ruchoo, started shedding tears. Ruchoo could sense that day that the tears were also the language of love. After that, he went towards the lamppost and touched the forehead of the bull with reverence and affection, the bull continued to munch fodder in a good temper. The night had fully descended, and within half an hour, all three of them were lost in the valley of sleep amidst the music played by nocturnal insects performing their night duty. If the day is good, a person gets a sound, soothing sleep during the night, too. Ruchoo was sleeping under the Rickshaw, the rickshawman was sleeping on the seat of the Rickshaw, and the bull under the lamppost. The rickshawman got up early, even before the Sun rose, and left his rickshaw to finish his morning tasks. Soon, Ruchoo too got up. Ruchoo, by shaking and stretching its body, was getting ready for the struggle for another day. It threw a glance towards the bull and saw that it was snoring soundly like a champion sleeper. Soon, the rickshawman came with his hand full, and it appeared that he had taken a bath and was ready for another day's struggle.

'Take Babua, I've brought some biscuits for you' said rickshwman placing a packet of biscuit on a paper. With that he also moved his hands on Ruchoo's back with affection.

Then he went towards the bull, saying, 'See, O' Bull of Lord Shiva, I've brought something for you too,' said the rickshawman, spreading a bundle of green grass before the bull respectfully. All three members of the victor team were enjoying their morning breakfast- the rickshawman taking poha and sipping tea on the seat of the Rickshaw, Ruchoo taking the biscuits under the Rickshaw, and the bull munching the green fodder under the lamppost.

The rickshawman was singing some devotional song in his local dialect, and both Ruchoo and the bull sat silently as if listening to the rickshawman's music attentively with rapt attention.

Soon, their brief span of peace and joy was disturbed by the gang of sweepers.

'Move your rickshaw from this place,' commanded one of the sweepers by pointing his sharp and rough broom at him.

'First, you clean that part of the road, by that time we'll finish our breakfast,' said the rickshawman to the leader of the gang confidently.

'Oh, rickshawman, this road is not your personal property. Move your Rickshaw at once, we don't have time to listen to your advise,' said one of the members of the sweeper gang rudely.

The rickshawman gestured to Ruchoo by saying, 'O' Babua, teach these people some politeness and courtesy.'

This was enough for Ruchoo, and it came out from under the rickshaw and, growling ferociously, jumped at one of the members of the Sweeper Gang. This sudden and unlikely attack from this unlikely corner forced the members of Sweepers to run away quickly from there in fear.

'Don't know why a poor man is a poor man's foe,' said the rickshawman, looking gratefully at Ruchoo as if asking for its opinion. On the other side of the overbridge, sweepers while sweeping the road were muttering almost inaudibly, 'Today the municipal people will root out this menace forever by throwing stray dogs out of the town, then we'll see this rickshawman and take our revenge'.

Ruchoo got upset on hearing it, particularly his anxiety and fear for the members of his team, who were innocent street stray dogs and easily vulnerable to being caught by municipal workers. Yesterday, Ruchoo had heard about the campaign by the municipal workers to catch stray dogs from various people, and the feeling of being a victor of the fight of the last night had completely disappeared as it prepared to face the new challenge to save itself and its members from being caught by the municipality.

Rickshawman was unaware of this campaign, and Ruchoo could not communicate its anxiety or fear to the rickshawman. It could not even tell the bull about this problem. So now it was clear that Ruchoo would have to deal with this problem on its own resources single-handedly. Then Ruchoo remembered that it is not alone in this fight, as there are three to four dogs of its team, also of whom Ruchoo was the leader. For a good leader, the safety and security of his team come first and foremost. The very next moment, Ruchoo moved towards its area after leaving the overbridge. It could not spot its team members in the lane where Ramdin's house was situated, so Ruchoo went to neighbouring streets too and messaged its team members by barking in a particular way. Animals' way of communication with their fellow beings is different from that of human beings, who communicate through a language.

Getting the message, all team members of Ruchoo, who were wandering in diverse streets, collected at once on a call from their leader. Ruchoo, like a good leader, knew the need to boost the morale of its team in times of crisis, not to terrify them by exaggerating the situation. Ruchoo's gestures were followed by the members in word and spirit, without any question or doubt, as they had full confidence in their leader. In the next half an hour, Ruchoo made a quick round of all the lanes, spotting the hiding places with its preening eyes that could be used in times of crisis. Besides, Ruchoo's alert and quick ears were ready to locate any signs of crisis. It appeared to members of its team that Ruchoo was looking for food, and Ruchoo did not reveal its true intention and allowing team members to spot any leftover food thrown by the residents of the streets.

On the main road, Ruchoo stopped at the cobbler's shop, who gave it biscuits and chapati to eat with affection. Though Ruchoo took it gratefully but after eating it, Ruchoo did not stay there for long as some voices of 'Catch, catch' accompanied by the noise of the engine of the tractor fell on its sharp ears. Ruchoo comprehended at once that the municipal team with a campaign to catch stray street dogs has finally come. It also saw four to five dogs running in diverse directions, followed by municipal workers shouting, 'Catch them, stop them.'

The tractor driver diverted the attention of the workers by pointing towards Ruchoo. Four people with poles and nets in their hands jumped from the tractor at once and came towards Ruchoo. But Ruchoo was quite alert and swift, and poorly fed municipal workers were no match for him in speed. Ruchoo had already sent its team members to safe hiding places. Ruchoo also saw that in the trolley, a cage was placed in which half a dozen unfortunate victims of this campaign were looking utterly helpless. Ruchoo was already prepared for this situation, and it ran towards the street where Ramdin's house was situated. Ruchoo also knew that its team members were not so alert and swift, so it had already advised them to go to safe hiding places.

The peace of the residents of the street was disturbed due to the noise made by shouting municipal workers who were chasing the dogs. On hearing the noise, Usha, wife of Ramdin, also came out of the house along with other women of the street. Seeing the chase, she uttered, 'It is good, worthless municipality has given thought to this menace and decided to take action on it.' Thus, Usha in a single sentence praised as well as condemned the municipality and its workers.

'Oh, it is just a sham, they are doing it as an eyewash just to fool people, as elections are nearing, that is why their spell of sleep has broken,' said a woman from across the street, giving her expert opinion. All other women nodded in approval.

'It is utterly surprising that dogs coming towards this side have disappeared suddenly. Where have they gone?' said a municipal worker in total disbelief, looking on all sides. Ruchoo with its team were hiding under a car that was covered on all sides by a canvas cover, so they could not be seen by the chasing man. Suddenly, one of the members of Ruchoo's team, unwittingly, put out its tail from under the cover. It was seen by Usha, who quickly pointed towards that direction, asking workers to move in that direction by saying, 'See the tail of a dog hiding under the cover of the car.' Ruchoo got enraged both at Usha and the foolishness of its team member, who was a lean and thin undernourished dog. So, without wasting time, Ruchoo and its friends left that place. Municipal workers ran after them, shouting 'Catch, catch, there they are' and succeeded in grabbing a spectre-thin member of their team. Ruchoo heard the helpless cry of this cur, and soon it turned around after pointing the other members to run towards the playground and hide at diverse places. As municipal workers were trying to bind their catch, Ruchoo made an onslaught on them. Ruchoo could have injured the worker by biting his hand, but his main intention was to rescue its team member from their clutches. So, they had no option but to leave their catch, and soon both Ruchoo and the spectre-thin member of its team were running towards the playground to safety.

'How rascal these dogs are,' commented a passerby woman who was watching the scene.

'Yes, these dogs are rascals for sure, but municipal workers should have come better prepared for such a situation.' Commented Usha, wife of

Ramdin, condemning the Municipal team. Meanwhile, Ruchoo had brought its entire team to safety as Ruchoo shared that after its attack, the campaign will take place on the streets only and not on the playing field where Ruchoo and its team members were hiding, as there were plenty of hiding spots in the playground and several ways to escape.

After some time, Ruchoo saw a tractor with captive dogs moving back, which indicated that at least for today, their campaign was over. Ruchoo saw the going tractor from behind a bush where it was hiding from the catching team. After some time, Ruchoo and its members saw a tractor passing before the playground with several dogs, looking miserably from behind the bars. Ruchoo also located those dogs who had challenged it a few days ago were also behind bars. A lean and thin member of its team expressed joy by barking at seeing those rival dogs behind the bars. Ruchoo quickly reprimanded this member for being a dog when it considered other dogs as its foes. Other creatures, including human beings, take advantage of this lack of unity among the beasts. Then a question came to Ruchoo's mind, why do human beings become a foe of other human beings when the Almighty Creator has created a wonderful food chain for every creature to survive.

'Some rascal dogs have escaped,' a voice from the tractor carrying captive curs fell on Ruchoo's ears.

'Don't worry, we'll come back after a few days again and punish all the rascals by catching them. But first of all, we will have to leave these in the forest, miles away from the town' said another person, pointing towards the captive dogs in the cage.

Ruchoo heaved a sigh of relief as these words fell on its ears. For at least some time, they can move freely in the streets without any fear, though they will have to remain alert, as this campaign may be resumed, seeing the upcoming elections, soon. It was also possible that these men may forget this campaign forever, as Usha, Ramdin's wife, felt that the municipal workers were worthless, who shirked from doing their duty properly. Soon, all the dogs moved towards that lane where there was a possibility of getting food. The sun was shining brightly in the sky, and the Sunlight appeared pleasant in the moderate winter season.

Now Ruchoo came towards the old, invalid cobbler friend. After finishing his meals, cobbler was closing his tiffin, when his eyes saw Ruchoo coming towards him, wagging its tail. Reopening his tiffin, he placed a roti and leftover vegetables before it happily. Ruchoo was feeling weary after a long day of stress and tension of running and saving its friends, so it accepted the cobbler's offerings gratefully and started taking them.

The sound of the school bell indicated to Ruchoo that school was over and it would be able to meet its young friends.

'Oh, there is our Ruchoo,' said Rahul, drawing the attention of the other kids towards Ruchoo.

'Thank God, Ruchoo is fine, I was praying to Almighty the whole day to keep Ruchoo safe and secure by making his escape attempt successful,' said Ronak, embracing Ruchoo with affection.

'Nobody can touch Ruchoo till I'm alive,' said the old Ccbbler enthusiastically, which threw a smile on everybody's face. After that, children proceeded towards their homes, but only after giving the leftover extra food from their tiffin boxes to Ruchoo and also with a promise to return in the evening to play on the ground. So now Ruchoo's tummy was full.

Over the last few days, the mothers of the children were pleasantly surprised to see a surge in the appetite of their kids as they were demanding extra food in their tiffins, let alone bringing home an unfinished tiffin box. Children have kept the fact related to Ruchoo a secret. Ruchoo came with their children till it came before Ramdin's house, where Usha, seeing it, uttered with disgust,

'Oh, where has this dog come from! Why nothing for good municipal fellows have left it!'

'Mommy, see it is our Ruchoo, reared and trained by Papa,' said Ronak, trying to explain to his mother meekly. But Usha was enraged, and at the same time, a motorbike came and stopped at one end of the street. It was the Municipal Councillor of that area who tried to talk sweetly to Usha.

'Madam, good day, today we had a Stray Dog Catch Campaign by the Municipality'

'Then what is it in front of you, a lion?' remarked Usha sarcastically to the Councillor.

'Don't be angry, lady, in two to four days we'll have another phase of the campaign to free the entire town from these stray street dogs. Our men will certainly take care of these creatures, you only care for me in the elections by voting in my favour' addressed the Councillor to Usha in a meek and pleading voice, and looking down on Ruchoo in disgust, he ignited his motorcycle and moved on. Ruchoo could not comprehend Usha's hatred towards dogs. On one hand, Ramdin took care of Ruchoo as his child, while on the other hand, his wife, Usha, did not want Ruchoo to live peacefully even in the streets. Ruchoo did not know what god had in store for its future yet, what troubles and crises it would have to face in its struggle to survive. Ronak and Rahul looked at Ruchoo helplessly as they entered their house. In their eyes, Ruchoo could read the invitation to play Cricket in the evening on the ground. It was still a couple of hours before Children would again come out of their houses to play in the evening. So Ruchoo decided to go back to cobbler for a while to pass his time.

As Ruchoo was about to come out of the street, a high-speed bike nearly collided with it, if Ruchoo had not been alert to move out of its way in time. But still Ruchoo barked at the bike rider as a protest. Two people were riding this speeding motorbike, and at the very first glance, Ruchoo's sixth sense that something was wrong with these bike riders as they appeared to be criminal and abnormal sort of characters. If its nose had been normal, it would have easily detected their intention. As Ruchoo was thinking about them, the bikers stopped in front of Chintu's house for a few moments, and after looking around for some time, they moved away at high speed, leaving a dark trail of smoke from the exhaust pipe of their bike. In the past, Ruchoo had caught several criminals, and just by looking at their faces, it could tell that their intentions were not good, so seeing these bikers, it grew suspicious of them too. But the problem was that it could not be about the nature of crime and the time when they intend to commit that crime. Ruchoo stayed there for some more time and, finding everything normal and in order, moved and came to the side of the old invalid cobbler and exhibited its talent to a number of customers who came to his shop. But still, he was apprehensive about the motor bikers who came at high speed and stopped before Chintu's house unusually. It was also apprehensive about the resumption of the municipality's efforts to catch stray dogs on the street. Though there was peace everywhere but Ruchoo did not know whether it was the permanent peace or peace before a storm.

However, Ruchoo still went to play with the kids in the evening. Kids were happy that Ruchoo succeeded in escaping municipal authorities, and so they were enjoying the game fully without any fear of some dreadful incident that might take place soon. But Ruchoo's eyes and ears got alert the moment it heard a motorbike. As he was more concerned about the safety and security so today it could not concentrate fully on the game, which even affected its performance in the field as it dropped several catches.

Ronak anticipated by saying, 'Perhaps Ruchoo is either tired or unwell today.'

'Let us take Ruchoo to Vet Doctor Uncle,' suggested Chintu while throwing the ball towards Ronak.

'Today we'll wait and see, if things do not improve, then we will trouble Doctor Uncle,' uttered Ronak, throwing a glance towards Ruchoo. Ruchoo was thinking if it could tell its worries and anxieties to the children. But then, on second thought, it chose not to disturb its friends by putting them into fears and anxieties like a true leader by telling them about it.

After the game was over, the children went to their homes. Ruchoo took a quick round of the lanes to ascertain peace and order in its area, It was trying to visualise the nature of crime that the bikers intended to commit in this area. But finding nothing unusual or alarming, Ruchoo returned to the rickshawman, who welcomed it as if he had met his close acquaintance after a long time, and Ruchoo also showed affection for him by wagging its tail while the bull was still munching unconcerned about the events taking place around it.

The darkness of the evening had descended in the sky. A distant moon was accompanied by a few smiling stars in the firmament, and the rickshawman, after taking his meals, was humming some tune of his favourite song in his local Bhojpuri dialect. As night advanced, the rickshawman went into a deep and sound sleep amidst the music played by the nocturnal insects. The bull also had gone down the peaceful dale of sleep by closing its eyes, but sleep was miles away from Ruchoo's eyes, though it did not know the specific reason for it. Suddenly, an idea struck Ruchoo whether these bikers had come to recce Chintu's house to commit burglary at the house during the night or day. On getting this thought, Ruchoo came out from under the rickshaw silently so as not to disturb the rickshawman and the bull and took a round of Chintu's street. The entire lane was vacant; nobody was either entering it or leaving the street. Ruchoo also looked at other houses too but found nothing suspicious. Ruchoo also found the members of its gang sleeping peacefully under a lamppost. Seeing Ruchoo there, they quickly collected around their leader. Ruchoo gestured to them to be alert during the night and warn them if they saw anything unusual or suspicious in the street, especially alert about any beggars. Every member of Ruchoo's team nodded in approval, and after that, Ruchoo went back to the rickshaw to sleep for the rest of the night.

The next morning, after getting up, Ruchoo again took a round of the street of Ramdin and, finding everything normal, returned. Seeing Ruchoo coming, rickshawman spoke, 'Babua, where had you gone so early without taking breakfast, and offered a few biscuits and Poha on the paper to it. Soon, the town too awakened as the loud and harsh noise of the traffic on the highway increased. Life in the town was coming into rhythm for the new day. After finishing breakfast, Ruchoo took another round of the lanes of its area, and then it decided to go to the Snack Vendor's shop.

The lorry of the Snack Vendor was crowded as usual. Suddenly, Ruchoo's eyes spotted a bike standing at some distance that looked identical to the bike that it had seen yesterday. Ruchoo saw that the crowd standing around the Snack Vendor Shop consisted of three to four kids, a few girls, and some adults who were buying snacks from the Vendor. Among them, Ruchoo also saw a familiar face of a young man who looked like one of the bikers, though his appearance was different from yesterday. Now Ruchoo recognised the man at once as one of the bikers, but was unable to spot another biker among the crowd. Ruchoo kept a close watch on the activities of this young man. He went to the Vendor to buy a couple of Samosas and returned towards the bike. Seeing a mighty hound like Ruchoo near the bike, he seemed to be upset for some time, but quickly normalised himself and he started the bike and moved away. Ruchoo could read something suspicious and wrong in the behaviour of this young man. Ruchoo decided to chase that bike, which was moving towards the playground. Though Ruchoo was following it but it kept a safe distance so as not to arouse any suspicion in him of being chased. Soon, Ruchoo also reached the playing ground and found that the motorbike was parked near a dark car at one of the corners of the ground, under the shadow of a tree. Ruchoo was keeping a close watch on their activities without arousing any suspicion in them that they were being observed. Motorbiker opened the door of the car, where three people were already sitting inside. Suddenly, Ruchoo saw that the driver of the car was none other than the second biker, whom Ruchoo had seen peering into Chintu's house a day earlier. Ruchoo was certain that they were planning to commit some crime, but how to know whether they were planning to commit some theft, burglary, or some other crime.

For the next ten minutes car's door remained closed and nobody came out. After half an hour, Ruchoo saw two men walking towards the dark car. Now Ruchoo was certain that it was a gang of five to seven people who came to town intending to commit some crime. After some time, two men came out of the car, and they were the same people whom Ruchoo saw yesterday. They took the motorbike and rode away. After some time, the car also moved away from that place, but strangely, they moved in diverse directions. Ruchoo was uncertain at first whether to chase the motorbike or the car, but then it decided to pursue the car that reached Ramdin's street at a high speed. For a moment, it slowed down before Chintu's house, but it did not stop altogether but it moved on rapidly. It came out of the main street to move towards the main road. Ruchoo was continuously after this car, but it stopped chasing the car after he reached the old cobbler's shop. By that time, Ruchoo was certain that these people were recceing the area to commit some crime, but what would be nature of the crime was still uncertain.

'Oh, Ruchoo, come here, my brave son,' called old cobbler affectionately, but Ruchoo was too preoccupied with its thoughts to pay any attention to the cobbler, and it went on to take another round of the area. The old cobbler was taken aback and somewhat sad at the strange indifference of Ruchoo towards him, but as a customer had come so he got busy dealing with the customer. Meanwhile, Ruchoo went to inspect Ramdin's lane carefully, and all the members of its team were cooperating with Ruchoo in its mission. The lean and spectre-thin dogs of its team welcomed Ruchoo by lying prostrate at its feet. As Ruchoo had decided to prevent the potential crime with the help of its team, it instructed the members of its team not to leave the street today and asked them to report any untoward and unusual development to Ruchoo immediately. The thin dog was put on duty right before Chintu's house. Currently street was almost vacant with very few people in it, as children were at school at this time of the day and menfolk would be at their work, so only women and a few senior citizens would be present in most of the houses at present. Ruchoo, after ensuring peace and delegating duties to the members of its team, went back to spend some time with the old invalid cobbler and took meals offered by the cobbler gratefully. For the next couple of hours, everything was normal, but Ruchoo's eyes were constantly towards the entrance of the street containing Chintu's house, and got alert at the sound of a motorbike. At one time, it even appeared to Ruchoo that perhaps it had committed a mistake by taking normal people to be criminals, and no such undesirable incident was going to take place.

Suddenly, the humming of the engine of the motorbike fell on Ruchoo's ears. As the motorbike became visible, it was out at once that it was the same motorbike that it had seen a day earlier before Chintu's house. Ruchoo got up at once and went after the bike and found that it had stopped at the far end of the street near an electric pole. While Ruchoo was trying to analyse the situation, the sound of the school bell signalled the end of the school which meant that soon children would come onto the street on the way from the school to their homes. Ruchoo gestured to its team members to be alert and follow its instructions. The young man riding the motorcycle did not turn off the running engine of his bike. One of the riders was talking on the cellphone while the other was looking around cautiously, and signs of nervousness could easily be discerned on the face of that man.

Ruchoo heard the children's voices as they entered the lane, and Ruchoo saw that just behind them, the same dark car slowly entered the lane that Ruchoo had seen in the playground. Ruchoo's alert mind did not take long to comprehend that these people were not going to commit theft, but they were after the children in their bid to perhaps kidnap some child. Children were talking among themselves and laughing, imitating the gestures of some of their teachers at school. Suddenly car stopped, and two men came out of the car, got hold of Chintu, and by pushing other children, tried to put him in the car.

Ruchoo took a quick leap with lightning speed and straight away entered the gate of the car. Following their leader, the other members of its team also got active as one of them ran after bikers, as the thin dog tried to stop the car by coming before it, but the car recklessly went over its feet as it cried in intense pain.

Entering the car, Ruchoo straight away bit the hand of the person holding Chintu. Men in the car were suddenly taken aback by this sudden attack of the dogs unexpectedly, as they had not considered the canine factor while planning their conspiracy. Ronak, Rahul, and other kids started shouting and crying, and soon there was chaos everywhere in the street. Meanwhile, Ruchoo, after biting the hand of the person holding Chintu, also assaulted the driver with its sturdy paws, as a result of which the car lost its balance and collided with the electric pole with a loud bang, and its doors opened. The other members of Ruchoo's team had rounded up the bikers and were threatening to attack them by barking furiously at them and by forming a ring around them. In this environment of chaos, all the residents came out after listening to the bang of the collision of the car, and by the loud shouting and cries of the children and barking of the dogs. It was a coincidence that Ramdin was also at home on leave that day, and he also came out of the house and soon rounded up the culprits in the car while other people nabbed other criminals who were trying to run away. Seeing Randin, Ruchoo was filled with joy and zeal and wagged its tail with affection as Ramdin embraced Ruchoo. Suddenly, Usha also appeared with Chintu's mother. Somebody in the crowd informed the police authorities, and soon a police van came to nab the culprits.

Today, Usha looked at Ruchoo with affection and regret for her past behaviour towards it. Apprehensively, she moved her hand on the hand and back of Ruchoo with affection that made Ruchoo forget all its ill feelings and mistreatment towards it in a moment. Now Ruchoo turned Ramdin's attention towards its member, whose leg had come under the wheel of the car and was shrieking loudly due to the sharp pain in its leg as it was bleeding profusely. That lean dog was taken to the Vet Clinic at once by Ramdin and a few other members of the colony. In

another hour, Ruchoo's acts of bravery and courage that averted an abduction bid spread throughout the town like wildfire. All the journalists, cameramen, leaders, and officers assembled at Ramdin's street to felicitate Ruchoo, who had become a celebrity and hero of the town due to its acts of courage and bravery. All cameramen were busy taking different poses of Ruchoo, and it too was obliging them like some celebrity.

The Municipal Councillor of the area, who also came, greeted Usha by folding his hands.

'Greetings, Madam, that day you were very much correct by calling Ruchoo a lion, as it has proved by its acts of bravery and courage that it is nothing less than a lion.'

Usha was listening silently to the Councillor as he proceeded, 'But don't worry, Madam, we'll start the campaign to catch stray dogs from tomorrow.

'Beware, even if you touch my dear Ruchoo or its companions. They are member of our family now.' said Usha in a warning voice to the Councillor. This statement of Usha was reverberated by the shouts of joy from Ronak, Rahul, and even their father Ramdin, who was happy to see the change of attitude in Usha towards Ruchoo. Ramdin declared happily, 'Next week, it will be time to celebrate Diwali, and we'll celebrate the festival of joy and light with Ruchoo and its team members.'

There was an atmosphere of joy in the street, and the thin dog had also returned from the clinic after getting its leg bandaged and receiving treatment.

It was a coincidence that the rickshawman, the friend of Ruchoo, took it in his rickshaw. Seeing Ruchoo there, he exclaimed joyfully, 'Oh Babua, what are you doing here?' When the children related the whole incident to the rickshawman, he also related an incident in which Ruchoo had saved him from hooligans. Seeing the crowd, the old invalid cobbler also came by, taking a lift from someone.

'I'll put up a proposal before the General Board of Municipality to honour and felicitate Ruchoo at Diwali for its acts of bravery and courage', said the Councillor as he put a piece of sweet in his mouth given by Usha.

'That means our Ruchoo will be the hero of Diwali,' said Rahul gleefully.

'This year, the joys of Diwali Celebrations will be doubled.' Chintu expressed his opinion enthusiastically.

For Ruchoo, this moment was just like the climax scene of some Bollywood movie ending happily for everybody. Today, its period of struggle was over as Ramdin took back into his family, and

Ruchoo got an entire family besides the admirers, both in the human world as well as in the brute world. The rickshawman from Bihar, crippled old cobbler, children of the colony, and its team members became an integral part of Ruchoo's family. Now Ruchoo was the hero of the town, though it had lost its sniffing power, yet it had gained an altogether new world in the form of new friends. Ronak started Diwali celebrations right then by bursting a cracker that terrified Ruchoo a bit, as it was an explosion, but everybody laughed at seeing Ruchoo apprehensive.

'Oh, our hero Ruchoo gets afraid too,' said Usha, embracing Ruchoo affectionately.

For Ruchoo, it was like getting the entire world.

----------End----------------